Contents

FOLK TALES FROM ASIA
FOR CHILDREN EVERYWHERE

Book Six

sponsored by the
Asian Cultural Centre for Unesco

New York · WEATHERHILL/HEIBONSHA · *Tokyo*

This is the sixth volume of Asian folk tales to be published under the Asian Copublication Programme carried out, in cooperation with Unesco, by the Asian Cultural Centre for Unesco / Tokyo Book Development Centre. The stories have been selected and, with the editorial help of the publishers, edited by a five-country central editorial board in consultation with the Unesco member states in Asia.

First edition, 1977

Jointly published by John Weatherhill, Inc., of New York and Tokyo, with editorial offices at 7-6-13 Roppongi, Minato-ku, Tokyo 106, Japan; and Heibonsha, Tokyo. Copyright © 1977 by the Asian Cultural Centre for Unesco / Tokyo Book Development Centre, 6 Fukuro-machi, Shinjuku-ku, Tokyo 162. Printed in Japan.

LIBRARY OF CONGRESS CATALOGING IN PUBLICATION DATA: Main entry under title: Folk tales from Asia for children everywhere / Book 3-: lacks series statement / "Sponsored by the Asian Cultural Centre for Unesco" / SUMMARY: A multi-volume collection of traditional folk tales from various Asian countries illustrated by native artists / 1. Tales, Asian / [1. Folklore—Asian] / I. Yunesuko Ajia Bunka Sentā / PZ8.1F717 / 398.2′095 [E] / 74-82605 / ISBN 0-8348-1037-9

T 405230

KOREA

Darling Sun and Darling Moon

Once upon a time a poor woman and her young son and daughter lived all by themselves in a remote valley. The children's father had died while they were still babies, and their mother had to work at other people's houses in order to support the family.

One day the mother said: "My children, you must make sure that the door is always closed and locked when I'm not here, and you must never open it for any stranger. They say that recently a huge fierce tiger has been coming down to the village disguised as a human being."

Early the next morning the mother left the house to go and help prepare a feast at the home of a rich man who lived ten hills away. She worked very hard all day. The sun was setting over the mountains to the west when she finally finished her job of grinding rice into tasty cakes mixed with sweet sesame oil.

Now, the rich man's wife was very generous. When the mother was ready to go home, the wife wrapped nine large cakes in a bundle and told the mother to take them home to her lonely children.

"I must hurry home with these cakes before they get cold," the mother told herself, "because the children must be hungry." And she went hurrying toward home as fast as she could, holding the bundle of cakes under one arm and happily thinking how joyful her children would be when she gave them the cakes.

But she'd worked so late that night fell before she had crossed the first hill. And yet she was not afraid because in her imagination she could see the star-bright eyes of her children lighting up like so

5

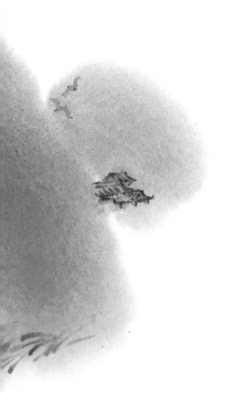

many lanterns. And then, all of a sudden, she heard a strange gust of wind and there before her stood a huge dark animal. It was the tiger!

"Hey," called the tiger, "what's that in the bundle you're carrying so tightly? It smells good. Give it to me, or else it will be you that I eat."

The mother was so frightened that she almost fainted. But she gathered up her courage and said: "Please let me go. These rice cakes are for my children's supper. They've been waiting all day without anything to eat."

But the fierce tiger was without mercy. "And what about me?" he said. "I too have been without food all day, so I'll just eat you up." And he was about to jump on the mother. She barely managed to escape by giving him one of the rice cakes.

Away the mother went running, hurrying toward home. But she had just arrived at the second hill when the tiger jumped out at her again and said: "You must give me one more cake and then I'll let you go."

So she gave him a second cake and then hurried on toward home. But the more he ate, the more the tiger wanted. He jumped out at the mother at each hill and

demanded another cake, until finally, at the ninth hill, she had
to give him the very last rice cake.

She sighed, with tears in her eyes, saying: "My poor children
will have to go to sleep hungry tonight."

Just as she arrived at the last hill, out jumped the greedy tiger
again and cried: "I'm still hungry! Now it's your turn to be
eaten!" And without another word the cruel tiger ate the mother
up. Then he put on the mother's clothes and went walking toward
the house where the children were waiting.

In the house the brother and sister were cold and hungry and afraid. They'd waited and waited and waited, but still their mother hadn't come back.

"Brother," said the girl, "I'm so hungry! Why doesn't Mother come home?"

"She'll be here soon," answered the brother. "Maybe she's late because she's bringing us a lot to eat."

The boy was doing his best to comfort his sister, but he too was on the point of tears. Just then there was a knock at the door and a voice said: "This is your mother. Open the door."

"Oh, it's Mother! It's Mother!" shouted the sister with joy, and she was about to open the door. But suddenly her brother stopped her, saying: "Wait a minute. It's a rather strange voice, don't you think?"

Then the children called out: "What's the matter with your voice? Our mother's voice is much more gentle and tender."

"I've been working hard all day and walking through the night and I feel tired, that's all," said the tiger with the sweetest voice he could make. "That's why I have such a hoarse voice. Quick, open the door."

The girl said: "Then push your hands in so we can see if they are our mother's."

When the tiger showed his hairy paws, the girl said: "But our mother's hands are much smoother than that. Why are your hands so rough?"

"Well, you see, I've been doing hard, rough work all day, so it's only natural that my hands should become scratched and rough. Besides, I was in such a hurry to come home that I forgot to wash them. If you're still suspicious, have a look at my clothes."

With that the tiger pushed part of his skirt into the crack of the door. It was their mother's skirt, no doubt about it. So the children opened the door.

The tiger went directly to the kitchen, saying: "Wait here, my children, and I'll get your dinner for you."

The tiger intended to take off the mother's clothes so he could move fast and eat the children up in one swallow. But they happened to see the tiger's long tail hanging out from under the skirt.

"Hurry! hurry!" the boy said to his sister, taking her by the hand. They slipped out the front door into the yard. A big tree grew beside the well there and they quickly climbed it and, holding their breath, hid among its leaves.

After undressing, the tiger leaped into the room to eat the children, but he couldn't find them anywhere. "Where could those silly children have gone?" he asked himself. He looked harder and harder, but he couldn't find a trace of the children.

"This is really strange. But I'll find them yet. First, however, I must have a drink of water and then I'll search some more."

The tiger went outside to the well and was beginning to draw up some water when suddenly he saw the forms of the children in the tree reflected in the water.

In a flash the tiger began to climb the tree, but its trunk was so smooth that he kept slipping back to the ground. "Dear children," he called, "how did you manage to climb the tree?"

The children answered: "We did it by oiling our feet."

Believing what they said, the foolish tiger hurried into the kitchen and put oil all over his claws. But then he found it even more difficult to climb the tree.

The sister was so amused by the tiger's foolishness that she forgot the danger and said to her brother: "Isn't the tiger silly? He doesn't even know that he could climb the tree easily if he cut steps into it with an ax."

But the tiger overheard the girl's words and began climbling with an ax. The children climbed higher and higher, trying to escape, and at last reached a small branch beyond which it was impossible to climb. Then the children prayed to the King of Heaven: "O King, please help us! If you will heed our prayer and save us, please throw us a strong rope. But if you will not save us, then throw us a rotten rope."

Hardly had they finished their prayer when a strong new rope came down from heaven. They managed to pull themselves up onto the rope just as the tiger reached the top of the tree. He couldn't reach them!

Frustrated and angry, the tiger cried to the King of Heaven: "Hurry and throw me a rope too," and again a rope came down from heaven. Without so much as a word of thanks, the tiger jumped on the rope and felt it flying up into the sky, with him still holding fast. But this rope was old and rotten, and soon it broke in two. The tiger fell back to earth, dead and bleeding.

When the children safely reached the Kingdom of Heaven, the king said to the boy: "You, my darling, shall become the sun." And he said to the girl: "And you, my darling, shall become the moon."

And so they did. But after a day the darling sister moon became unhappy because she was afraid to stay outside in the dark all night long. So the darling brother sun changed places with his sister.

As the sun the girl was happy because she could walk in the bright light of day, but she was embarrassed as well because people on earth kept staring at her. Then her brother suggested that she send the dazzling sunlight down to earth. She did as her brother told her, and sure enough, people quit looking at her.

And that's the way it still is. We can look at the moon all we want, but the sun is much too bright for us to look at. And it also happened that the place where the tiger fell bleeding to earth was

a large field of the kind of grain called sorghum. And that's the reason why, to this very day, the heads of sorghum are still blood red.

Retold by Hyo-seon O
Translated by Sang-jun Lee
Illustrated by Kwang-bae Kim

The Goat and the Wolf

Once upon a time there was a Chinese goat, the kind with two horns on its head that sometimes you can see and sometimes you can't see. She was a mother goat, and she had three children, whose names were Hakak, Pukak, and little Kulula Sangak.

One day the mother went out to look for food for her children. While she was gone a wolf stole into her house and gobbled up all three children.

When the mother returned home, she couldn't find her children anywhere. Filled with sorrow, she sat down and thought about what might have happened. Suddenly she remembered the wolf.

Quickly the mother went running to the wolf's house. She climbed up on top of the roof and began pounding with her hooves.

The wolf cried out from inside the house: "Who's that shaking my roof and scattering dust over my guests' food? The food is all dirty and my guests have been blinded by the dust."

The mother answered: "I am the Chinese goat with two horns

on my head that sometimes you can see and sometimes you can't see. Now tell me who ate my Hakak? Who ate my Pukak? And who ate my little Kulula Sangak?"

The wolf answered: "I ate your Hakak. I ate your Pukak. And I ate your little Kulula Sangak."

The goat said: "Tomorrow you and I will fight."

The wolf said: "Very good, tomorrow we'll fight."

The goat went home and filled a bowl with milk. Early next morning she took the milk to the blacksmith. She said to him: "That wicked wolf has eaten my three children. Please sharpen my horns, because after lunch today there's going to be a fight

between me and the wolf. I've brought you this bowl of milk to pay you for your trouble."

The blacksmith took the milk, and then he sharpened the goat's horns until they were as sharp as daggers.

Presently the wicked wolf also came to the blacksmith's shop. He brought with him a sack filled with stones and dirt. He said to the blacksmith: "Please sharpen my teeth, because after lunch today there's going to be a fight between me and the Chinese goat. I've brought you this sack of food to pay you for your trouble."

But when the blacksmith looked into the sack, he could see nothing but stones and dirt. He became angry, and when the wolf opened his mouth, the blacksmith only pretended to sharpen his teeth and instead pulled them all out. Finally he said: "There, now your teeth are sharp."

After lunch the wolf and the Chinese goat stood facing each other, ready to fight. The wolf called: "You attack first!" The goat answered: "You attack first!"

Then the wolf opened his mouth and charged at the goat, ready to tear her stomach open. But he had no teeth and couldn't so much as nip her.

Then it was the goat's turn. Lowering her head, she ran at the wolf. Her sharp, sharp horns went right into the wolf's stomach

and tore it open. Out of the wolf's belly stepped Hakak. Out stepped Pukak. And out stepped little Kulula Sangak.

Overjoyed to see her children safe and sound, the goat washed their faces, and then they went happily home. After that they all lived happy, happy lives—the Chinese goat—and Hakak—and Pukak—and little Kulula Sangak.

Translated by Aziz Ahmad Yusofzai
Illustrated by Mohammad Hashim

The Kidnapped Boy

One dark night long, long ago, in the southern part of the island called Sulwesi, a shadow stole quietly out of a house. It was the figure of a man carrying something heavy on his back. Surely the man was a thief, but what was it he carried? Finally, when he reached the edge of the forest, the thief put his burden down on the ground, and it turned out to be a young boy who had just reached his teens.

"You'll have to do your own walking now," the thief said roughly to the boy.

The boy had been kidnapped from his father's home, and he realized that the kidnapper meant to sell him as a slave, as was often done with young boys in those days.

"Go on, get a move on!" hissed the thief, giving the boy a shove.

The boy got up slowly and followed the man farther into the forest. How he longed to run away and go home to his mother and father, but only the kidnapper knew the way through the blackness of the great old trees. Realizing he was helpless, the boy put his life into the hands of fate and began trying to think what he should do. He racked his brains so hard that he even forgot the bruises on his arms and legs. At last, after much thinking, the boy hit upon a plan.

Suddenly he stopped walking and, clutching his stomach tightly, squatted on the ground.

The man turned around and said: "Get on your feet or I'll beat you!"

But the boy stayed squatting on the ground and looked up at

the man piteously. "I can't," he whimpered. "My stomach aches so badly I can't move."

"Can't you even walk?" asked the man.

The boy shook his head, looking as if the pain was still stronger. "You'll just have to carry me. I really can't take another step with this pain."

"Oh, all right," grumbled the man. "But quit your crying and keep quiet."

So the boy climbed on the man's back, glad that the first part of his plan was working. The man kept on walking, and after a while the boy kicked his legs against the man's side.

"What is it now, you little pest?" asked the man.

"Please, won't you tell me a story?" said the boy. "Then my stomach won't hurt so much."

"Tell you a story? While I'm carrying such a load? Oh, very well."

The boy smiled secretly to himself. It was just what he wanted. The man would have a hard time keeping up his fast pace with the boy on his back if he tried to tell a story at the same time.

"Do you know," began the thief, "that all these great big trees are nothing compared to the big tree in my story? It's even bigger than all the trees in the world tied together."

The boy gave a groan and the man said: "Is your stupid stomach still hurting?"

"I can hardly bear it—but please go on."

"Well, at the same time there was a giant ax, the biggest ax in all the world. One end of it was in the east, where the sun rises, and the other end was in the west, where the sun sets. . . . Hey! How's your stomach now?

"Oh, it's still aching, but please go on."

"Well, there was once a giant water buffalo, bigger than the

whole wide world. When it moved just the tiniest bit, the earth would shake and tremble. That's what makes earth-quakes."

"Oh, oh, my poor stomach!"

"Shut up, you spoiled brat. Now I'm going to tell you about a long, long piece of rattan."

"Rattan?"

24

"Yes, the kind of palm vine used, like rope, for tying things. And this piece of rattan was so very, very long that it could encircle seven lands and seven seas. . . . You're awfully quiet all of a sudden. How come?" asked the man, looking back at the boy on his back.

"Your story is so very interesting," answered the boy, but actually he wasn't believing a word the man said.

"Once," continued the man, "there was the biggest house you ever saw. It was so big and so high that if someone threw a chicken egg from its roof, the egg would hatch and grow into a grown chicken before it reached the ground."

"My!" exclaimed the boy, "what a house! . . . Now it's my turn to tell you a story." The boy was still following his plan of escape.

"All right," said the man. "But how's your stomachache now?"

"It's a little better, thank you, and I think it will go away entirely if I tell you a story as well."

"Good! Start your story, then."

"Well, my story is about a very big drum that was used long, long ago. It was so huge that everyone in the world, even up to the gods and angels in heaven, could hear it roar when someone beat it."

"Oh, that's nonsense!" broke in the man. "There could never be a drum that big."

"Why not?"

"Where would people have found enough wood to make such a drum? And even if they found a huge tree, what could they have chopped it down with?"

The man was panting by now, so he put the boy on the ground and told him they were going to have a little rest. The boy smiled secretly: his plan was working better and better.

"Well?" asked the man.

"Oh, that's easy. They would have gotten the wood from the great big tree you told me about, which was bigger than all the trees in the world put together, and they would have chopped it down with the giant ax with one end in the east, where the sun rises, and the other in the west, where the sun sets. That's what you told me, isn't it?"

The kidnapper was becoming annoyed. "All right, so they chopped down the giant tree with the giant ax. But I still say it's nonsense. Where could they have found a skin big enough to cover the drum?

"Oh, that's easy too. You told me about the giant water buffalo bigger than the whole wide world, which caused earthquakes by moving just the tiniest bit. Its skin would be wide enough to cover the drum, wouldn't it?"

"And how could it be tied around the drum?"

"Why, they used the long piece of rattan you told me about, the rattan that could encircle seven lands and seven seas."

The big man with the little brain did not want to be outwitted by this small boy, so he said again: "All right, that's possible so far, I guess. But how about telling me where they could hang a drum as big as that?"

"In your giant house, which was so tall that if anyone threw an egg from the roof, it would hatch and grow into a grown chicken before it reached the ground."

The man couldn't think of anything else to say. He was surprised by how smart the boy was. "It's as if he's giving my own stories back to me," he thought to himself. Then, pretending to forget all about the stories, he asked the boy: "Do you have brothers and sisters?"

"Yes, my older brother has two younger brothers, and one of them has two older brothers. So how many brothers have I got and what number am I among them?"

"Huh?" was all the stupid man could find to say.

"It's simple really. My parents have three sons and I'm the second. So the younger brothers of my older brother are my younger brother and myself. And the older brothers of my younger brother are my elder brother and me."

By now the kidnapper had realized that the boy had outwitted him. "He's worn me out already," he thought to himself, "and it would be dangerous to keep him with me." So he decided to take the boy back to his parents.

Back he went, then, taking the smart little boy home, and the boy was smiling to himself in the dark of the night.

As soon as he had returned the boy, the kidnapper stole quickly out of the house again, and with a sigh of relief, he disappeared into the dark forest.

Retold by Sagimun M. D.
Translated by Ati N. Hadimadja
Illustrated by Irsam

The Dog Who Wanted to Be the Sun

Once there was a little dog named Greenie. He thought he was smarter than all other dogs. He thought and thought and looked at the sun. He looked at the sun every day until he grew up. And still he kept looking at the sun, forgetting himself in deep thought.

The other dogs were puzzled. "Why do you keep looking at the sun?" they asked him.

"I want to be the sun," Greenie replied. "Why can't I be the sun instead of him, and let the sun be a dog?"

An old dog said: "The sun is good to all of us. He is just and kind and shines on us all. How could you be the sun? You don't even know how to shine."

"I can shine better than he can," said Greenie, "and I want to be the sun." Then he looked up at the sun and said: "Do you hear me, Sun? Come down here and be a dog in my place, and I'll be the sun."

It was late afternoon, and the sun was gradully coming down from the sky. He was golden red and bright, and was beaming at all the creatures on earth. He said: "I hear you, Greenie. What is it you want?"

"I want you to be a dog in my place."

"But there has to be a sun to shine on earth."

"You think you're so fine and mighty!" answered Greenie angrily. "You're the stupidest sun I ever saw."

"Listen to me, friend Greenie," said the sun. "We all have to do our duty. My duty is to shine on the earth. And I am the sun by nature. You are a dog by nature, and your duty is to be the best dog you can. If we both do our duty, then we'll both be happy."

"I know all that," said the dog. "Of course someone has to shine on the earth. And I can do it best. So I want to be the sun."

The sun was silent for a time, thinking deeply. Finally he said: "All right. From now on you can be the sun, and I'll be a dog in your place."

So Greenie became the sun. He did his duty and shone brightly. He also decided that he should bring justice to the world. So he shone fiercely and ruthlessly on anyone or anything that he thought should be destroyed. Many people were killed by his fierce rays, but he was pleased because he was destroying evil and diseases and germs upon the earth.

But people couldn't understand what was happening. The dog-sun kept on working hard, shining strictly and brightly. And before long everyone felt too hot. Everyone, both people and animals, had to dig holes and live in them to escape the sun's terrible heat. Some of them went to the king and said: "We're in trouble.

32

Since the dog became the sun, the world is too hot and we can't live natural lives but have to live in holes like ants."

"I do too," said the king, and he scurried back into his hole out of fear of the dog-sun.

Then the people and animals went to see the sun-dog who used to shine on them. They cried angrily: "It's your fault! You've let the dog take your place and you no longer do your duty. Now the dog-sun shines so fiercely that many of us have died and the rest live like ants."

"But things look all right, don't they?" asked the sun-dog.

"They may look all right to you," said an old dog, "but they're not. Things are quiet but not serene. We all live in fear. Our way of life is now too strict and stern. We're afraid of the dog-sun and have to hide in holes. No one smiles any more."

"Be patient," said the sun-dog. "Happiness depends upon the way you think. Nature takes care of everything. Believe me, my friends, all's well that ends well. If you have confidence in the great truths of life, you'll be happy. Just look into the sky and see what's happened."

They looked up and saw that a big, thick cloud, the biggest and thickest anyone had ever seen, had come between the dog-sun and the earth so he couldn't shine fiercely any more.

The dog-sun became very angry and cried out loudly down to the earth: "Where are you, Sun? Come back here. You can be the sun as before; I want to be a cloud."

"All right," said the sun, beaming and climbing up the sky as he used to do every day. "You can be a cloud."

Then the dog became a big, thick cloud and stayed between the earth and the sun. The sun couldn't shine upon the earth, and everything was in darkness. Everyone was troubled and shouted to the sun: "It's your fault!"

Suddenly a strong wind came blowing through the sky. It blew so hard that the cloud was broken into tiny pieces.

"I don't want to be a cloud any longer," yelled the dog. "I want to be the wind."

"All right," said the sun, "you can be the wind."

Then the dog-wind blew and blew with all his might, so fast and hard that nothing could resist him. He broke to pieces everything that stood in his way, and for many days he enjoyed blowing and blowing.

But one day he saw something that stood still no matter how hard he blew. It was a hill of white ants that he simply couldn't blow down. So he demanded: "Now I want to be an anthill."

"All right," said the sun, "you can be an anthill."

So the dog became an anthill and felt very strong. But one day

a water buffalo came running across the anthill, and beneath its pounding hooves the anthill crumbled into dust.

Then the cloud of dust flew to the sun and demanded: "I want to be a water buffalo. Let me be what I want!"

"All right," said the sun, "you can be a water buffalo."

Then the water buffalo went running along destroying every anthill in sight and being very pleased with himself. But one day a farmer's son saw the animal and threw a loop of rope over its horns and captured the water buffalo, tying him to a big tree.

"Sun!" cried the dog-buffalo. "I want to be a mighty rope."

"All right," said the sun, beaming down upon the water buffalo. "You can be anything you want."

So the dog-buffalo became a rope. And then suddenly a brown puppy came running up to the rope. He was a playful puppy and

35

took the rope in his sharp teeth and shook it and pulled it and bit it and chewed it until the rope was all torn into tiny pieces. The brown puppy went running happily on its way.

Once more Greenie cried loudly to the sun: "I want to be a dog again."

"All right," said the sun, still beaming, "you can be a dog again."

And the rope became a small dog named Greenie, who went running about happily. And the soft breezes blew, whispering with the blades of grass in the fields of earth. And the sun went on shining every day.

Retold by Sunit Prabhasawat
Illustrated by Tepsiri Suksopa Group

The Owl and the Elephant

Once in a thick forest there lived an owl and an elephant who were close friends. For many years they had shared each other's joys and sorrows, and in times of trouble they always tried to help each other.

One day the elephant felt hungry and set out in search of food. Wandering deeper and deeper into the forest, he suddenly found himself in a gathering of demons. The demon king had just had a dream in which he had eaten an elephant. So the demons were delighted to find a real elephant standing in front of them and insisted that their king's dream must be made to come true. Then they grabbed the elephant and got ready to kill him. No matter how much he protested, they paid him no mind.

Finally the elephant said: "Please, then, let me have one last meeting with my oldest and dearest friend."

The demons agreed and the elephant promised faithfully that he would come back soon to be eaten. Then he set out to see his friend the owl.

Along the way the elephant asked everyone he met: "Is it really true that if you eat something in a dream, you must also eat it in real life?" Everyone assured him that this was true, and he went on his way feeling miserable and depressed.

Finally the elephant reached the tree where his friend lived and found the owl sitting calmly on a branch. With many sighs, the elephant told the owl what had happened and then said: "So goodbye, my dearest friend, I must go now to be eaten by the demon king."

"No, no," said the owl, "you mustn't despair. Let me come with you and I'll think of some way to save you."

So the two friends set out together for the demons' place. The company of his friend consoled the elephant. The owl rode perched on the elephant's head, because if he had used his wings to fly he would have arrived long before the elephant.

When they reached the gathering of demons, the owl pretended that he had just awakened from a deep sleep. He fluffed out his feathers and looked around with wide eyes at the assembled demons. Then he said: "I've just had an amazing dream in which I married the queen of demons. So I really must marry her. Where is she, then?"

But the demons protested loudly. They said: "You can't marry our queen just because you married her in some stupid dream."

Quickly the owl replied: "If I can't make my dreams come true, how is it that your king can insist on eating this elephant just because he ate one in a dream? If he insists on eating my friend, I too must insist on marrying your queen."

The demons were so dumbfounded that they didn't know what to say. So they let the owl and elephant go back to their homes, and this is the way the owl saved the life of his good friend the elephant.

Retold by Tulasi Diwasa
Illustrated by Madan Chitrakar

Singapura, the Lion City

Long, long ago the small island at the tip of the Malay Peninsula was called Temasek, as that was the name of the small village that was on the island. And this is the story of how the island's name came to be changed to Singapore.

Once there was a young rajah on the island of Sumatra who decided he wanted to establish a new city. He sent for his chief minister and said: "I have thought of a plan for building a new city. We could sail along the coasts and look for a good place. What do you think?"

"It shall be as Your Majesty pleases," the minister replied. "If Your Highness goes exploring, I shall go too."

So orders were given, and soon a large fleet of ships was ready to sail. There was a golden ship for the rajah and his retainers. There was a silver ship for his wife and her ladies-in-waiting. There were ships for the ministers and ships for the war chiefs. So great was the number of ships that the sea could hardly be seen when the fleet finally set sail.

News of the fleet quickly reached the island of Bentan, which was ruled by a queen, or rani, who was rich and powerful. She sent her ministers out in ships to welcome the rajah and his fleet and invite him to visit Bentan.

Now, the rani had no husband and, not having met the rajah before, she thought he might make a good husband for her. But when he arrived on the island, she found that he was many years younger than she and that he already had a wife. So she decided to adopt him instead as her son. He came to live in the palace with her, and she gradually grew so fond of him that she said he should be the next ruler of Bentan after her.

After the rajah had been in Bentan for a time, he asked the rani's permission to go on a hunting expedition to another island. At first, the rani was reluctant to let him go. She could not understand why he wanted to go to the other island to hunt when Bentan was full of deer and chevrotains and porcupines for hunting. But when she saw how restless and unhappy the rajah was, she finally agreed to let him go and supplied him with as many ships and men as he needed.

The party set sail and presently reached the other island. They went ashore for a picnic on the sandy beach. The rajah's wife and her ladies-in-waiting enjoyed themselves gathering shellfish and mangrove flowers and seaweed, while the rajah and his men went hunting. They were quite successful.

During the hunt the rajah saw a deer and followed it for some distance. The deer tried to escape, but the rajah was able to spear it. Near the place where the deer died there was a huge rock.

The rajah climbed to the top of the rock. Before him there stretched the ocean, and far in the distance he could see a strip of pure white sand, the beach of yet another island.

Struck by the beauty of the scene, the rajah said to one of his ministers: "Look at that beautiful island. What is it called?"

The minister answered: "That's the island of Temasek, Your Majesty."

"I'd like to go there," said the rajah.

"It shall be as Your Majesty pleases," replied the minister, and he immediately gave orders for the rajah's ship to be made ready.

The rajah and his ministers embarked and set sail for Temasek. But no sooner were they on the open sea than a storm arose.

43

Mountainous waves broke over the ship, which soon began to fill with water.

All the crew and the ministers began bailing the water out of the ship, but they soon realized that more water was coming in than they could bail out. The ship was in danger of sinking. So the captain ordered that the ship be lightened, and they threw all their heavy luggage overboard.

But still the ship was about to sink. "Everything that can be moved must be thrown overboard," cried the captain. And they threw overboard everything else they could lay their hands on.

The ship was now near Temasek, but still it was about to sink. "Whatever can I do?" the captain asked himself. "I'm sure we've thrown overboard everything we can." He looked about to see if there was anything else that could go. Just then the rajah turned toward him and a jewel in the rajah's heavy crown glinted in a ray of sunlight.

"The crown!" the captain said to himself. "The rajah's crown! That must be the cause of all our trouble. It's the only thing left that can be thrown overboard. But what can I do about it?"

The captain kept wondering what to do, but finally, when he saw the ship was really about to sink, he plucked up courage and said: "Your Highness, it seems to me that it is because of your crown that our ship is sinking. Everything else has been thrown overboard. If we don't do the same with the crown, we'll all die in the sea. May I humbly suggest that Your Highness throw the crown overboard?"

The rajah did not hesitate or protest. "Into the water with it, then," he said, throwing the crown into the raging waters.

Immediately the storm stopped. The ship floated well once more and sailed smoothly toward Temasek. Without any trouble, the ship was brought in close to the shore and everyone landed safely.

It was indeed a beautiful island! For a time the rajah and his men amused themselves collecting shellfish. But the rajah soon tired of this and decided to go inland for a hunt.

While they were hunting they suddenly saw a majestic animal that moved with great speed. The beast had a reddish body and blackish head and mane. Its belly was tawny. It was much larger than a goat and very sturdy in build.

When the animal saw the rajah and his party, it showed no fear of them but turned its head gracefully to look at them and then walked away slowly.

"What animal is that?" the rajah asked. "I've never seen one like it before, have you?"

No one could tell him, but one of the ministers said: "No, I've never before seen an animal like that, Your Highness, but I've been told that in ancient times the king of beasts looked like that. I think the animal we saw just now must have been a lion."

The hunting party continued on to the small village on the island, where they spent some days. Finally one day the rajah remembered his original plan and called his ministers together. "I shall establish my new city here on the beautiful island of Temasek," he announced. Then, turning to one of them, he said: "Go back to Bentan and tell the rani that I shall not be returning and that, if she still has affection for me, she will show it by supplying me with men and elephants and horses so we can build a city here."

The minister took the message to the rani, who agreed to help, saying: "I shall never oppose any wish of my son."

So she sent men and elephants and horses in such great numbers that the rajah was easily able to build the city he had so often dreamed about.

Finally the city was finished and it was time to give it a name.

The rajah remembered the beast he had seen. "Ah! That's what I'll call this new city of mine—Singapura, which means Lion City. It shall become a great city, as great among cities as the lion is great among beasts."

So they named the city Singapura, and as the years went by, the rajah's words came true. Singapura—or Singapore, as it is often called today—indeed became a great city among the cities of the world. People from other countries came in large numbers to live there, and soon the fame of the city and its greatness spread throughout the world.

Retold by Violet Wilkins
Illustrated by George Paul

How to Share Five Cakes

Once upon a time there was a farmer who, some time earlier, had married off his two daughters. One day he decided to pay his daughters a visit to see how they were getting along.

First he went to see the younger daughter, as she had married only recently. She had been wooed by a rich man, but the farmer had refused him because, he said, his family was not good enough. So she had eventually married a man who, though of good family, was very poor, and now she lived in poverty. Her clothes were cheap and ragged, and she and the other members of her husband's family lived from hand to mouth.

When her father arrived, she invited him to have a seat and then pretended to get some food ready for him. But there was no food in the house and all she did was place a pan on the fire and

put into it some old, dry tamarind seeds, which are not at all fit to eat. She kept stirring the seeds, and when they began to roast they made a sound like "Kas, kas, kas."

"Whatever are you roasting?" asked her father, curious.

Now, the daughter was still angry because she'd been made to marry such a poor man. She said: "Since we don't have any money, Father, we sometimes have to cook the only thing we have —my husband's good family name."

The farmer felt insulted by his daughter's words. Without even replying, he rose and left the house and started off for his other daughter's place. Now, the older daughter had been married to a rich man and was very well off. When the father reached her house, his daughter treated him with great consideration, the way he thought a child should act to show gratitude to a parent. After making him comfortable, she set to work and made him some special cakes out of rolled rice pastry that was a great delicacy in her village. Her father found the cakes delicious and asked what they were called. The daughter answered: "They're called vella vahum," which is a name that means something like "sweet-rice-dough."

After he'd eaten his fill, the farmer set out for home, beaming with satisfaction and hurrying as fast as he could. He kept muttering to himself: "Sweet-rice-dough, sweet-rice-dough," so he wouldn't forget the name.

Along he went, jiggety-jig and joggety-jog, sometimes leaning forward as he ran loping and sometimes leaning to the side, but always to the tune of "Sweet-rice-dough, sweet-rice-dough." He passed some girls going to market and smiled at them to the tune "Sweet-rice-dough, sweet-rice-dough." People along the way thought it very funny to see the old farmer hurrying along singing "Sweet-rice-dough, sweet-rice-dough." Had he gone weak in the head? Was he taking leave of his senses? But the old man ignored all the curious glances and rude stares. Whenever he met anyone he knew, he'd give the customary greeting: "I wish you long life," and add: "Sweet-rice-dough, sweet-rice-dough."

Hurry! hurry! hurry! And the faster the old farmer went, the more he wobbled. Suddenly he stubbed his toe against a big rock and cried out in pain: "Oh my toe! Oh my toe!" But he kept going, hopping and limping and sometimes stopping to rub his foot. And he kept saying: "Oh my toe, oh my toe." Somehow he had unconsciously replaced the name "sweet-rice-dough" with this new refrain.

When he finally reached home and limped to his chair, he had no sooner seated himself than he said to his old wife: "Our daughter made me some delicious oh-my-toe, which is a specialty of her village. You too must make me some oh-my-toe because I'm very fond of it."

"Whatever is oh-my-toe?" the old woman answered. "I never heard of such a thing in my life!"

"What a fine wife you are! Here I'm over sixty years old and in all our years together you've never made me any oh-my-toe! It's a disgrace! Your own daughter can make oh-my-toe, but you— you've never even heard the name!"

"And in all our years together, I've never heard a good word from you," shrilled the wife. "Nag, nag, nag! You've never appreciated anything I've done for you. What an ungrateful husband!"

"Out of my house, you old hag!" stormed the farmer.

Their quarrel grew louder and louder until all the neighbors were looking in the windows. One of the neighbors, watching the way the old woman looked as she quarreled, said: "She rolls her lip up till she looks like a cake of sweet-rice-dough."

"That's it! that's it!" cried the old farmer jubilantly. "That's what I meant—sweet-rice-dough!"

So the quarrel ended as quickly as it had begun. The old woman knew very well how to make sweet-rice-dough, and she set to work immediately to make some for her husband.

When the wife had finished making five cakes of sweet-rice-dough, the farmer said: "Fine—three cakes for me and two for you."

But the old woman served him only two of the cakes, keeping three for herself. This raised another storm, and they started abusing each other until they were shouting loudly.

"If you'd only shut your big mouth," shouted the farmer, "we could sit and enjoy our cakes."

"My big mouth!" screamed the wife. "And what of your big, big mouth?"

"You should stop your shrieking out of respect for your mother's memory," the man shouted.

Then for a moment there was complete silence. Finally the farmer said: "Now, isn't this silence wonderful? Let's make a bet: whoever breaks the silence and speaks will get the smaller number of cakes."

"You'll be the one to break it!" retorted his wife.

"Then let's bet!" said the husband.

"Done!" said the wife.

So there the two of them sat at the table with the five cakes before them, and neither of them would say a word. Noon wore into evening and evening into night, but not a word did they utter. In silence they went to bed.

Next morning, the silence continued. The farmer and his wife lay in separate beds, making not a sound, not a whisper. Occasionally they would speak in sign language about whatever had to

be done, but not a word was said. Thus the days passed and the cakes stayed uneaten on the table, and the daily chores stayed undone. The food they had in the house began to run out, and neither of them would tell the other to go get more. Finally they were too weak even to speak in sign language, and they took to their beds for good. The neighbors and

friends had been so used to the sound of quarreling from the farmer's house that they became worried by the silence. They came to the house to see what was wrong and found the old man and woman lying motionless in their beds. The people came into the house and prodded them, but still they would not speak. They lay as if deaf and dumb.

The people decided the old couple must be dead, and they got ready to bury them, and still the old man and woman would not utter a word. The people dug two graves and began to lower the bodies into them. As they were lowering the farmer, someone dropped a shovel and it landed right on the old man's sore toe.

He simply couldn't stand the pain. "Oh my toe!" he cried loudly.

Up rose the old woman, dressed in her grave clothes. She cried: "I've won! It's you who broke the silence, and the three cakes of sweet-rice-dough are mine—all mine!"

Indeed it was the old woman who had won the bet. . . . And that, my dears, is the difference between sweet-rice-dough and oh-my-toe. Please don't ever forget.

Retold by D. Walatara
Illustrated by Somasiri Herath

Editor's Note. This story, known as "Vella Vahum" in Sri Lanka, is a simplification of Mr. Walatara's version.